First published 1996 by Verlag St. Gabriel, Mödling,
Vienna, Austria, under the title ZWEI UND MEHR

First U.S. publication 1998 by The Millbrook Press, Inc.,
2 Old New Milford Road, Brookfield, CT 06804

Printed in Austria

2   4   5   3   1

Library of Congress Cataloging-in-Publication Data
Fuchshuber, Annegert.
[Zwei und mehr. English]
Two peas in a pod / Annegert Fuchshuber.
p.   cm.
Summary: Twin boys and a number of animal families
express their uniqueness and introduce the numbers from
one to ten as well as fifty and one hundred.
ISBN 0-7613-0410-X (lib. bdg.). — ISBN 0-7613-0339-1 (pbk.)
[1. Animals—Infancy—Fiction. 2. Mother and child—Fiction.
3. Individuality—Fiction. 4. Twins—Fiction. 5. Counting.] I. Title.
PZ7.F94Zw   1998
[E]—dc21   97-26944   CIP   AC

Two Peas

Annegert Fuchshuber

in a Pod

The Millbrook Press

Brookfield, Connecticut

Paul and Peter are twins. People say: "They are as alike as two peas in a pod." Their mother doesn't like to hear that. She says that her boys are very different from each other. She always knows which is which.

To make it easier for people to tell them apart, she has Paul wear red socks. Peter wears blue.

To make it more difficult for people to tell them apart, every once in a while Peter will wear red socks and Paul will wear blue.

Can you tell who is who?

Their mother can—but there are times, especially when they switch socks, she says that two are quite a handful.

"Handful?" asks Mama Bear.

"I adore my two! I think they make the perfect family.

"Some people say my little cubs are as alike as two peas in a pod, but really they are very different from each other. I love both of them very much.

"Of course, chasing two around the woods can be tiring, so I don't think I would want to have three."

"Why, that's ridiculous!" growls Papa Lion. "It takes only a look at my three darling cubs to see that three is just the right number.

"Some say that they are as alike as three peas in a pod, but to me they are all totally different.

"I think three is the perfect number of children, and my wife agrees. Four might be a worry."

"That makes no sense," says Mother Mole.

"Why would you only want to have three? Just three would bore me. My four may appear to be as alike as peas in a pod, but each one is special. I can tell them apart—even in the dark. And how much I love them all!"

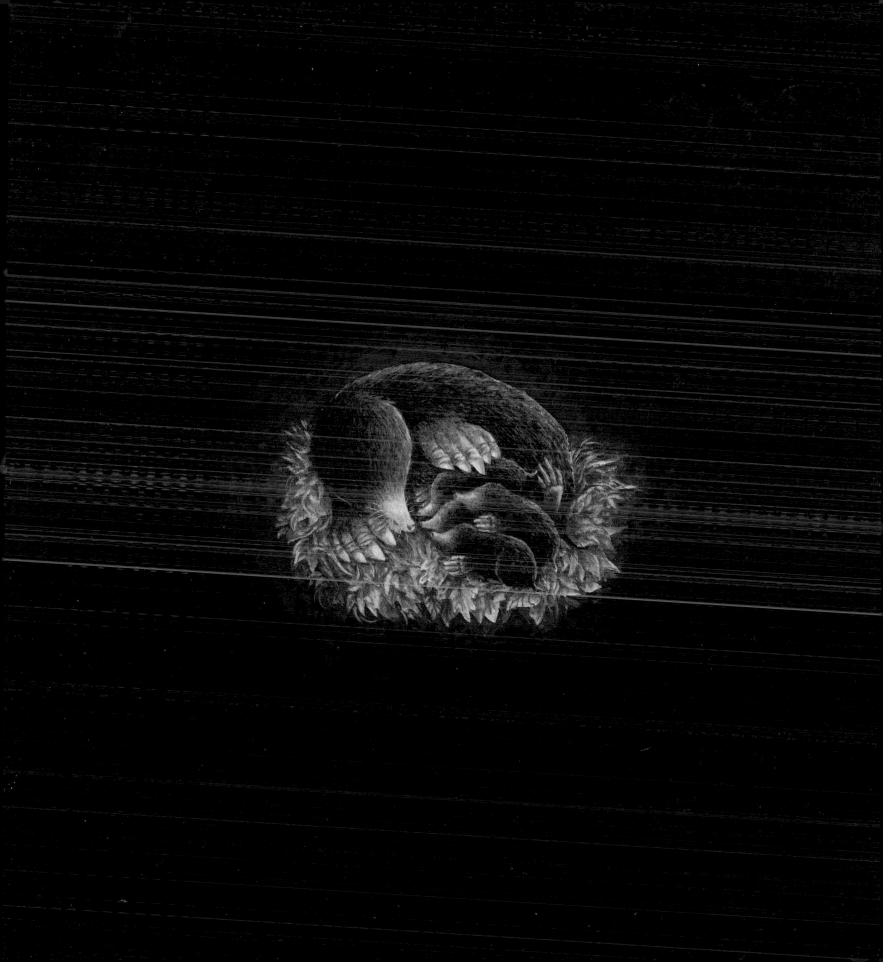

"Only four? That's not enough," says Mama Owl.

"If you can afford it, then why not have more?

"You might think mine look like peas in a pod, but when they hatch, I'll have a happy family of five.

"Each of them will sing its own owl song. Can't you just hear them cheeping?"

"Only five?" sneers Mother Cat.

"I'm a proud mother of six. Each kitten is cuter and cuddlier than the next. People who say they are as alike as peas in a pod can't see them as they are! Six are very easy to tell apart—though I admit that more might cause problems."

"Problems?" bristles Mother Hedgehog.

"I produced seven and I have had no problems at all with any of them. I just snort at strangers who think they're as alike as peas in a pod. That's nonsense. Each of my babies is special. Seven are heaven!"

"It's all a matter of feeding them right," squeaks Mother Mouse. "If you know what you're doing, it's easy to have eight. And I would be so lonely without my darling children.

"They all have different personalities, and it hurts me to know that some people think they are as alike as peas in a pod.

"My motto is 'eight is great!' Although I must admit that feeding more could be a challenge."

"It's not true," grunts Mama Wild Boar, "that eight is enough! To make a family whole it takes my nine sweet children.

"And as to the rumor that they look as alike as nine peas in a pod, it's absolutely not true. Each of them is special. I would not give up a single one of them! Nine is my lucky number."

"Nor could I give up any of my ten wonderful children. What a thought!" says Mrs. Rabbit. "I could never decide which one to give away. They are all such darlings, even if there are those that think they are as alike as peas in a pod. Ten is such a wonderful number that I'm thinking of having ten more!"

"Ten is nothing," hums old Mother Beetle. "Under fifty eggs would be a waste of my time.

"Each of my little babies is a unique individual. Aren't they all cute?

"I've heard the talk about peas in a pod, and since when are all the peas in a pod alike?

"Now I suppose I would have some difficulty if I had hatched more than one hundred little darlings."

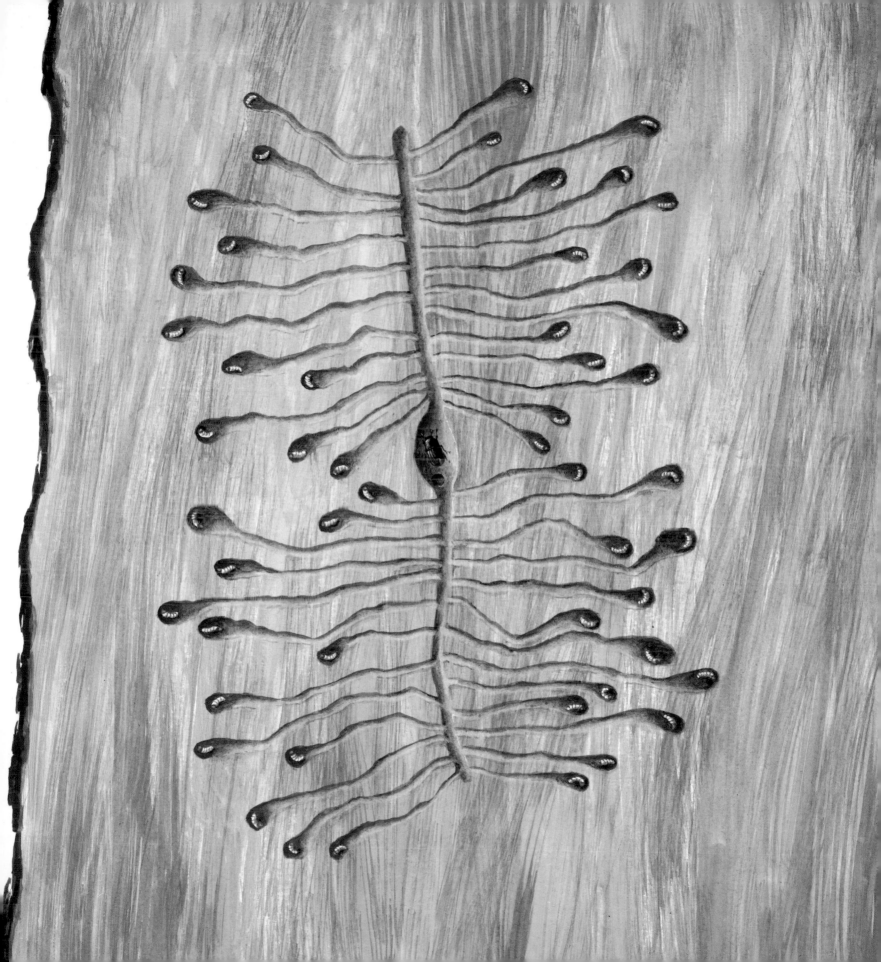

"Oh, my dear," croaks Mrs. Frog.
"Babies

cannot be too numerous. I don't even try to count my little

polliwogs. But I love each and every one of them, and I

watch them grow more beautiful every day.

"With children such as mine, why would I want to stop

at a hundred?"

"It's really a shame," says Paul.

"That we're only two," says Peter.

Or was it Paul who said that?

About the Author

Annegert Fuchshuber has been writing and illustrating books for many years. Her children's books have been translated into many languages and have been awarded a number of prizes, among them The German National Award for Literature for Children and Young People and The Austrian National Award for Literature for Children and Young People. Her English-language titles include *The Wishing Hat*, *A Mouse Tale/A Giant's Story*, *Cuckoo Clock Cuckoo*, and *The Pied Piper of Hamelin*.

Ms. Fuchshuber lives in Augsburg, Germany, with her architect husband and three children.